Guy Bass

ANNA GAIN

AND THE SAME SIXTY SECONDS

With illustrations by
Steve May

To Mario

First published in 2020 in Great Britain by
Barrington Stoke Ltd
18 Walker Street, Edinburgh, EH3 7LP

www.barringtonstoke.co.uk

Text © 2020 Guy Bass
Illustrations © 2020 Steve May

A CIP catalogue record for this book is available from the British Library upon request

ISBN: 978-1-78112-916-6

Printed in China by Leo

CONTENTS

Anna Gain

The strange tale of Anna Gain will only take a minute.

One minute. Sixty short seconds. For most of us, a minute seems to pass in no time. But for Anna Gain, one minute can last *for ever*.

All Anna cared about was being on time. No one was sure why.

Her father was a clockmaker. Every room in the house was full of clocks of all shapes and sizes. Anna's home ticked and tocked – was that why Anna thought so much about time?

"Every second counts," Anna's dad told her every day. Maybe *that* was why time mattered so much to her. Maybe it was because her little brother was late for *everything* and didn't seem to mind one bit. Or maybe Anna felt that if you were late, you might just miss out on something *wonderful*.

So Anna Gain always felt that she had to stay one step ahead of time, and that is exactly what she did. That is, until one hot Tuesday in late July ... the last day of school before the summer holidays, when the strange tale of Anna Gain began.

Chapter 1
The Tick-Tock of Time

"The bus is coming."

"You're going to be *late*," said Anna's little brother with a grin.

Anna checked her watch – the one with the red strap that showed hours, minutes and seconds.

"I'm never late," she said. She finished her last spoonful of cornflakes and put her bowl in the kitchen sink. From the kitchen window, Anna saw all the way to the top of the road. She spotted the school bus in the distance – the Number 13, right on time. Anna looked at her

3

little brother trying to pull on his right shoe without untying the laces. Then she checked her watch again. "Time's running out," she said. "The bus is coming. One more stop before ours ... that makes it 90 seconds away."

"And you're gonna miss it!" Anna's brother shouted. "You're gonna miss it cos I've—"

"Hidden my bag?" Anna asked.

"Hidden your ba— Wait, what?" blurted Anna's brother. "How did you know?"

"Because you *always* hide my bag," Anna said. "Every morning you hide it and hope I'll take so long looking for it that, for the first time *ever*, I'll miss the bus to school."

"You will today!" laughed Anna's brother. It was lucky for Anna that her brother only ever hid her bag in one of three places:

- the shoe cupboard, which was full of shoes, umbrellas and half-finished clocks;

- the gap under the stairs, which was full of half-empty cans of paint and half-finished clocks;

- the top of the fridge, which was, of course, covered in half-finished clocks.

"You're wasting your time. I always find it," said Anna as she checked the top of the fridge.

"So? I like wasting time," replied her brother, hopping into the hall after Anna with only one shoe on.

"Then you're getting it wrong," Anna tutted. "That's not what time's for."

"Time's not *for* anything," huffed Anna's brother. "You're always saying, 'Hurry up! You'll be late! Every second counts!' *Stupid* tick-tock, tick-tock! Why can't everything just take as long as it takes? Why do you want to be stuck counting every stupid second?"

"I'm not stuck, I'm one step ahead," Anna told him as she checked under the stairs. "Which is why I'm not going to waste any more time telling you not to waste time."

"That doesn't even make sense," said Anna's brother.

"Nor do you," Anna said as she looked in the shoe cupboard. "Aha!"

Anna pulled her school bag out from under all the shoes and made her way to the front door. As she grabbed the door handle, she spotted the time on her watch: 08:01:56.

A second later Anna's dad came out from his workshop carrying a half-mended clock.

"Make sure you catch that bus," he said. "Remember, every second counts ..."

Anna turned round. Her brother was still looking for his left shoe. She had spotted it under the stairs but she decided not to tell him. Anna smiled as she saw her brother begin to panic. She checked her watch.

"Every second counts," Anna said. With that, she turned the door handle and pulled open the door.

It was 8.02 a.m.

And it would be for a very long time.

Chapter 2
One Minute, Part One

"Hold the bus!"

As Anna's brother looked for his shoe, Anna stepped out of the front door. She took the three steps down the path to the front gate, being careful not to tread on Mrs Crimp's cat. Mrs Crimp lived eight houses away at Number 44 but her cat liked to curl up outside Anna's house and relax in the summer sunshine.

08:02:04.

"Morning, Pandora," Anna said, and stepped over the cat. "Mrs Crimp will be looking for you."

The cat purred.

A pigeon cooed from a nearby tree.

A blue butterfly fluttered over Anna's head as she heard the rumble of the Number 13 bus making its way down the road.

"It's a mornin' for yawnin'," someone called out. Anna spotted Old Mr Upshot on the other side of the street, walking his dopey Doberman. Mr Upshot nodded to Anna and smiled. Anna gave him a wave, swung open the front gate and stepped out onto the pavement.

08:02:10.

"Hi Anna see you at school sorry can't stop!" someone shouted. A girl from Anna's class darted along the pavement on a bicycle, pedalling for dear life. Anna shook her head as the girl raced past her.

Late Kate ... always late, Anna thought.
*If only she'd set off earlier. Better yet, why
doesn't she just take the bus? Late Kate never
learns ...*

Anna looked back at her house. The front
door was still open. Her brother had found his
other shoe and was trying to put it on.

Every second counts, Anna thought to
herself. She turned and looked up the road.
There was the Number 13 bus. All she needed
was 12 seconds to walk along the pavement
to the bus stop. She had time to spare. Anna
stepped forward ...

08:02:13.

In an instant, the same blue butterfly flew
past Anna's face. The tiny insect was so close
that Anna felt its wing tips brush the end of
her nose. With a squeak of surprise, Anna
stumbled backwards. Her right foot landed on
the cat's tail as it lay in the sunshine.

REEOW!

The cat leaped up and darted between Anna's legs. Anna just had time to cry, "Pandor—" before Mr Upshot's dog spotted the cat and barked loudly. The dog pulled hard on its lead and Mr Upshot dropped the lead in surprise. Mr Upshot's Doberman raced across the road after Mrs Crimp's cat. Before Anna knew what was happening, the dog jumped onto the pavement and ran past her, its lead flapping behind it like a cracking whip.

Without thinking, Anna grabbed the dog's lead.

08:02:19.

"Waah!" Anna screamed as Mr Upshot's Doberman began to drag her up the street. Anna saw the Number 13 bus pass her. "Oh, no ... Stop!" Anna yelled, digging her heels into the ground. The dog barked again as Mrs

Crimp's cat clawed its way up a tree and onto a branch.

08:02:28.

"Stop, stop, stop!" Anna screamed. She looked back as the Number 13 pulled up at the bus stop and she saw her brother running out of the house with his laces untied. He looked up the road and saw Anna.

08:02:35.

"Hold the bus!" Anna cried, clinging on to the lead as Mr Upshot's dog tried to climb up the tree after Mrs Crimp's cat. With a tug, Anna looped the lead around a nearby lamppost and tied it in a knot. But just then she heard the SHUFF of the bus's doors slide open. She turned again to see her brother get on.

Anna's brother was on the bus ... and she wasn't.

08:02:40.

Anna ran.

Chapter 3
The Second Thirty Seconds

"This can't be happening."

08:02:44.

Anna pelted down the pavement. She ran as fast as she could with her school bag banging on her back. She was twenty steps away when she saw the bus's doors close with a *SHFFFFFF*.

08:02:50.

"Waaaiiiit!" Anna panted. By now her brother had made his way to the back of the bus. Anna saw him press his face up against the back window and give her a wave.

The bus pulled away.

08:02:53.

"No ..." Anna gasped.

The bus lumbered down the road, turned a corner and was gone. Anna couldn't believe it. For the first time since she started school, she had missed the bus.

Anna was going to be late.

"This can't be happening," Anna snarled. Her face turned an angry hot red. "This. Can't. Be. Happening!"

08:02:56.

Anna squeezed her eyes shut and held her breath. "This *isn't* happening! Not to me! Do you hear me?" she screamed.

08:02:58.

"This! Isn't! Happening!" Anna cried again. *"This isn't—"*

08:03:00.

"Make sure you catch that bus," someone said. "Remember, every second counts ..."

It was her dad. He was right behind her.

"I can't catch the bus, it's gone!" Anna snapped, but her voice suddenly sounded different – as if she wasn't outside any more. Then Anna remembered that her eyes were still shut. She slowly opened them.

Anna was back *inside* her house. She was standing by the front door, her hand reaching out for the door handle.

"Wait ..." she muttered. *"What?"*

Chapter 4
The Same Sixty Seconds

"Is that the same butterfly?"

"I said, every second counts," Anna's dad said again.

Anna spun around. She was in the hall. Her dad stood at the other end, inspecting the same clock Anna had seen moments ago. Her brother was there too, digging around in the shoe cupboard as he looked for his left shoe.

"What's going on?" Anna asked. "How did I get here?"

"How did you *get* here?" replied Anna's dad. "Well, that's complicated, peanut – maybe ask your teacher when you get to school …"

"But I was outside," Anna said as she looked up and down the hallway. "I missed the bus …"

"Does that mean we don't have to go to school?" asked Anna's brother from the shoe cupboard.

"No, it does not," said her dad. "And you *can't* have missed the bus – I just saw it coming down the road."

"What …?" Anna turned back to the door and opened it. There was Mrs Crimp's cat lying in the middle of the front path.

"Pandora? How are you back here already?" Anna muttered. She walked slowly down the path and stepped over the cat as it purred. There was the coo of a pigeon in the tree further up the road – the very same tree that the cat climbed only seconds ago. Anna saw a blue butterfly flutter over her head.

Is that the same butterfly? Anna thought as she swung the gate open.

"It's a mornin' for yawnin' ..."

Anna looked up to see Old Mr Upshot on the other side of the street with his dopey Doberman.

"How did—?" Anna began. She peered up the street. There was the lamppost where she had tied up the dog only seconds ago. The dog wasn't there.

"Hi Anna see you at school sorry can't stop!" cried Late Kate as she sped past Anna on her bicycle. Just as she'd done a moment ago. Had Kate turned back? Had she forgotten something? What was she doing back here?

It was then Anna saw it – the Number 13 bus was making its way down the road.

"Wait, what?" Anna muttered. Her jaw fell open. "Is – is that a *different* bus?"

As Anna's mind raced, the blue butterfly suddenly fluttered into her face – again? Startled, Anna stumbled back.

REEOW!

Anna's foot had landed on the poor cat's tail. The cat jumped up and darted between Anna's legs.

A moment later there was a loud bark and Mr Upshot dropped his dog's lead. Anna watched the Doberman race across the road. She felt herself frozen to the spot as events played out exactly as they had only moments ago. Mr Upshot's Doberman raced past her house after Mrs Crimp's cat. Suddenly, it was as if everything was happening in slow motion.

Anna knew what to do – or did she know what she'd already done? She grabbed the lead. Straight away, the dog dragged Anna up the road, just as before. It pulled her along the pavement after Pandora until the cat climbed up a tree.

"I did this ... I just did this!" Anna said. By now her head was spinning so fast that she didn't see the Number 13 bus pass her as it made its way down the road. She didn't see it pull up at the bus stop. She didn't even see her brother race out of the house.

In fact, it was only when she heard the *SHUFF* of the bus's doors opening that Anna turned round and watched her brother climb onto the bus, just as before.

"Wait ..." she muttered as the bus's doors closed with a *SHFFF*. She saw her brother's face in the bus's back window. He gave her a wave.

"Wait!" Anna cried again, but too late – the bus pulled away and made its way down the road. It was as if Anna had re-lived the same sixty seconds. She checked her watch.

08:02:53.

It was not yet 08:03. But that was impossible, wasn't it? Anna looked around at everything that was oh-so the same as before. She shook her head and checked her watch again.

08:02:58.

"What's going on?" Anna gasped. "How did I end up back in the—"

08:03:00.

"Make sure you catch that bus," someone said. "Remember, every second counts ..."

It was her dad. He sounded like he was right behind her.

And there was the front door again – right in front of Anna's face. Her hand was reaching for the handle. Her watch showed 08:02:00.

She was back at home.

Again!

Chapter 5
Back in Time

"Not again!"

"Wait, what?" Anna muttered as she span around. There was her dad with the half-mended clock and her little brother digging around in the cupboard for his shoe. "How's this possible?"

"How is it possible that your brother always loses a shoe? Who knows?" her dad replied with a sigh. "And yet it happens every day, like clockwork."

"His shoe is under the stairs …" Anna said, her mind bursting with thoughts too strange for her brain.

"It is?" her brother said as he rushed out of the shoe cupboard to check. He found the shoe in a second. "How'd you know?"

"I saw it … before?" Anna said. She couldn't believe what she was saying. As her brother pulled on his shoe, Anna looked at her watch.

Still 08:02. Or was it 08:02 *again?* Something had happened that Anna could not work out – she had always felt one step ahead of time but now it seemed like time was taking a step back! It was then that Anna dared to ask herself a single mind-blowing question.

Had she gone *back in time?*

"Mrs Crimp's cat is outside!" she blurted, and quickly pulled open the door. Sure enough,

Pandora lay on the path in the morning sunshine.

"Isn't she always? Mrs Crimp will be looking for her, I expect," chuckled Anna's dad. Anna walked down the path. She stepped over the cat as if in a dream and opened the front gate. Everything had reset once more. Anna saw the blue butterfly ... heard the coo of the pigeon in the tree up the road ... spotted Old Mr Upshot ("It's a mornin' for yawnin'") walking his dopey Doberman ... and then Late Kate ("Hi Anna see you at school sorry can't stop!") zoomed past on her bicycle.

Anna knew what was going to happen next. So when the butterfly flew into her face, she did not flinch; instead of stumbling back onto the cat's tail, she simply wafted the butterfly away, her feet fixed to the ground. But then ...

"I'm ready first!" shouted Anna's brother. Because she'd told him where his shoe was, he'd already put it on and now he was racing to beat his sister to the bus stop. He ran out of the open door and down the path ... and his foot landed on the cat's tail.

With a *REEOW!* the cat screeched and darted between Anna's legs.

"Not *again!*" Anna cried. A moment later there was a loud bark and Mr Upshot dropped his dog's lead. Anna watched the Doberman race across the road. Anna froze to the spot as the moment played out just as she remembered. Mr Upshot's Doberman raced past her after Mrs Crimp's cat. Anna was about to grab the lead ... but then she saw it.

The Number 13 bus making its way down the road.

Was it grabbing the dog's lead that made me miss the bus? Anna thought. *What happens if I don't?*

Anna pushed her hands into her pockets and let the dog race past her. The cat darted left, then right, with Mr Upshot's Doberman on its tail.

"Stop him!" Mr Upshot suddenly cried, hobbling into the road. "Me dog's as soft as sponge cake! That cat'll have him for breakfast!"

Anna watched as Mr Upshot tripped on the kerb. He tried to right himself once, twice, three times – as if he was in the middle of an odd sort of dance – and then he tumbled into a helpless heap in the middle of the road.

It was 08:02:34 ... and the school bus was headed straight for Mr Upshot.

Chapter 6
Another Chance

"I've known hens that were less chicken than you!"

"Mr Upshot!" Anna cried. With the bus heading towards them, Anna rushed out into the road to where Mr Upshot had fallen over. Before Mr Upshot could remember his name, Anna grabbed the old man by his collar. "Move!" she screamed.

Anna dragged him to the side of the road and onto the pavement. She heard the squeak of dry brakes as the bus ground to a halt alongside them.

"Everything all right?" asked the bus driver.

Anna was about to beg him to wait for her when Mr Upshot cried, "It's my dog! If he corners that cat, it'll have his guts for garters and no mistake – he's got a bark worse than his bite, does that dog! I once saw him jump at the sight of a woodlouse. Imagine it, a dog afraid of a woodywig – a nutbug, a billy buttons! He's soft as soap suds ..."

The bus driver shook his head and started the bus up again. As the bus headed to the bus stop, Anna was about to cry, "Don't go without me!" but Mr Upshot had more to say.

"I might've been roadkill if not for you, lass!" he shouted as Anna helped him to his feet. "He's as dopey as a diplodocus, that dog – he can't even see his face in a puddle without getting scared!"

By now Anna wasn't listening. She saw her brother race past them on his way to the bus stop. He grinned at her and sped up.

"Sorry, Mr Upshot, I've got to go!" Anna shouted. She turned back as the bus pulled up at the bus stop. This time, Anna was only a few steps away. This was her chance ... Another chance!

She was going to make it.

"Ah, there he is! Come 'ere, boy!" declared Mr Upshot as the bus doors opened with a *SHUFF*.

"There *who* is ...?" Anna muttered. She had a split second to turn and see Mr Upshot's terrified Doberman racing back down the road towards her at speed, with Mrs Crimp's hissing cat chasing after him. "Oh n—!" was all Anna could utter before Mr Upshot's massive dog ran into her. Anna went flying. She crashed into Old Mr Upshot and both of them landed in a heap on the pavement. The dog jumped over them and kept on running, and a moment later Mrs Crimp's cat jumped on Anna's face as it tried to catch the dopey Doberman.

"Ow wow owww ..." Anna groaned. Suddenly everything felt like it was in slow motion again. Anna opened her eyes and saw the blue butterfly over her head. She felt as if she was dreaming.

"Dopey dog, get back 'ere!" snapped Mr Upshot. "I've known hens that were less chicken than you!"

"The bus ...!" Anna wailed as she tried to get up. Then came the *SHFFF* of closing doors. Anna looked up just in time to see her brother through the bus's back window. He was laughing and pointing at her. "Wait!" Anna cried, checking her watch.

08:02:53.

"Wait, wait, wait!" Anna shouted again. She got to her feet and ran after the bus. Moments later, the bus vanished down the road.

Anna Gain was going to be late.

Again!

"No!" Anna yelled. "This can't be happening again!"

"Are you all right?" asked Mr Upshot. Anna checked her watch.

08:02:57.

"This was my second chance!" she cried. *"This was my chance to—"*

08:03:00.

"Make sure you catch that bus," someone said. "Remember, every second counts ..."

Anna was inside the house again, standing by the front door. She was back where she started – or rather, *when* she started. Anna knew there was only one way to break the cycle ... only one way to escape the same sixty seconds. She glanced at her watch.

08:02:02.

"You look a bit ... tense," her dad said. "Are you OK, poppet?"

"I will be," Anna replied. "Just as soon as I catch that bus."

Chapter 7
The Pigeon

"Don't you dare send me back!"

Anna made sure *not* to tell her brother where his other shoe was and then pulled open the front door and marched down the front path.

"You stay right where you are, Pandora," she said, and stepped over her. Mrs Crimp's cat purred. The pigeon cooed. Anna swung open the front gate and stepped onto the pavement. The blue butterfly flew overhead.

"It's a mornin' for yawnin'," said Mr Upshot, on the other side of the street. His dopey Doberman hadn't even noticed Pandora yet.

Instead, he was happy to bark at a pigeon that was up in the tree further along the road.

"Things are ... different," Anna said. She took a step forward as she watched the pigeon fly out of the tree. "This is my chance to catch the—"

"Look out!" came a cry. Anna shrieked as Late Kate zoomed past on her bicycle, only just missing her.

"Sorry Anna see you at school can't stop!" shouted Late Kate.

That could've been worse ... and I'm still on track, thought Anna with a sigh of relief. She wafted the blue butterfly out of her face as she watched Late Kate speed down the pavement. Then she saw the pigeon from the tree glide right over Late Kate. A second later, Anna watched a brownish-white glob of pigeon poo fall from the sky and land with a *SPLUT* – right on Late Kate's head.

"Uh-oh," cried Anna as Late Kate's bicycle wobbled and swerved off the pavement into Mrs Crimp's front garden ... just as Mrs Crimp stepped out of her front door.

"Pandora! Brekkies, Pandora!" howled Mrs
Crimp. "Pandor—AAH!"

Mrs Crimp's howl echoed around the
street as Late Kate zoomed towards her on
her bicycle. Late Kate swerved at the last
second and rode straight into Mrs Crimp's
prize-winning – and very thorny – rose bush.

By the time Anna and Mrs Crimp had picked
Late Kate out of the rose bush and plucked out
the worst of the thorns, the Number 13 bus had
come and gone. Anna raced back down the
pavement to see her brother wave her off yet
again. She gave a sigh and checked her watch.

08:02:57.

"Don't you dare send me back!" Anna
screamed as the bus turned a corner and
vanished. "Don't you dare send me back to   "

08:03:00.

"Make sure you catch that bus," said her dad. "Remember, every second counts ..."

Sure enough, Anna was back in the house again. It was exactly 08:02.

"Argh!" Anna growled. "How does this keep happening?"

"You tell me," said Anna's dad with a sigh. "Why can't your brother just keep his shoes together in one place?"

"No, it's *time*! Time's messing me about and I won't have it! I don't care how long it takes ... I don't care how many times I have to go back," Anna growled. "I don't care how many minutes I have to go through! I will catch that bus!"

But 64 minutes later, Anna Gain was right back when she started.

Chapter 8
Anna Gives Up

"I'm going to be stuck in the same stupid sixty seconds for ever!"

Try as she might, Anna just could not catch the Number 13 bus. No matter what she did, *something* always stopped her. Between dogs and cats, butterflies and pigeons, Old Mr Upshot, Late Kate and Mrs Crimp's rose bush, it seemed like Anna was doomed. Again and again and again, Anna tried to get on that bus ... but every time she missed it and found herself back at home at 08:02 precisely.

"I can't take it any more!" Anna screamed as she stared at the front door after her 65th try at bus-catching. Her dad looked up from his half-mended clock.

"Anna Gain, what's got into you?" he asked.

"It doesn't make any difference what happens, I never catch it!" Anna howled, and threw her school bag to the floor. "I give up! This is my life now ... I'm going to be stuck in the same stupid sixty seconds for ever!"

"Dad, what's wrong with Anna?" whispered Anna's brother from inside the shoe cupboard.

"Who cares what I do? I always just end up back when I started!" Anna sobbed. She started to walk up and down the hall with her arms flapping like wings. "Look at me," she cried. "I'm a chicken! Buk-buk-bakaawwwwk!"

Anna clucked and squawked her way around the house. She knocked over chairs and stormed into the back garden with a "buk-buk-bakaaawk!"

"Can I be a chicken too, Dad?" asked Anna's brother.

"No, you cannot! Get on that bus!" his dad shouted as he marched into the back garden after Anna. "Anna, that's enough! What's got into you?"

"Maybe this is what time wants! Maybe time *wants* me to be a chicken!" Anna shouted. "Buk-buk-BAKAAWW—"

08:03:00.

"Make sure you catch that bus," said her dad. "Remember, every second counts ..."

"ARRRRRGH!" Anna yelled. She was back where she started *again* and her watch showed:

08:02:02.

"This is mad!" Anna shrieked. "It's a mad minute!"

"Anna, are you all right?" asked Anna's dad as he looked up from his half-mended clock.

"All right? I'm *great*! I can do whatever I want, look!" Anna screamed. She stamped into the kitchen and pulled open the fridge door. "I think I'm thirsty, maybe I'll have a drink!" she said. She took a bottle of milk out of the fridge. Then she took off the lid and poured the milk all over her head.

"Anna!" her dad cried.

"*Much* better! But now I'm a mess! Time for a *makeover*!" Anna grabbed a pen and began to draw a curly moustache on her face. "Perfect! I'll be sure to keep this fresh new look for, oh, I dunno, another few seconds!"

"Anna, stop!" cried Anna's dad.

"I! Wish! I! Could!" Anna screamed at the top of her lungs. "But I'm not done yet ..."

Chapter 9
Mad Minutes

"I'm Mary Poppins; I'm Mary Poppins!"

Over the next 78 minutes (or rather, over the same sixty seconds again and again) Anna Gain forgot about trying to catch her bus. Instead, she decided to have some fun. So Anna:

ate all the chocolate in the cupboard;

put on all of her clothes at once;

ripped up her homework;

did a handstand and sang "I'm A Little Teapot" upside down;

*barked like a dog as she drew a picture
of a barking dog on the wall;*

*juggled with shoes (it took fifty-two goes
to learn but Anna got rather good at it).*

Anna spent her 79th "mad" minute spinning an open umbrella around and shouting, "I'm Mary Poppins; I'm Mary Poppins!"

Her brother ducked but Anna's dad was not so quick – Anna's umbrella knocked his half-mended clock out of his hand and sent it flying across the hall. The clock smashed into the wall and broke into pieces.

"You're in trouble!" Anna's brother shouted.

"Anna, look what you've done!" snapped her dad.

"It doesn't matter! Nothing I do matters!" Anna yelled, and threw the umbrella on the floor. Anna pointed to her watch. "In a few seconds, it'll be like it never happened."

08:02:22.

"What do you mean?" asked Anna's dad.

"The clocks ... me ... everything. I keep trying to tell you, I'm going to be stuck in this minute *for ever*," she said. Anna slumped onto the floor and began to cry. "I was always one step ahead but now I can't stop going back."

08:02:31.

"Oh, poppet, is this about being on time?" said Anna's dad as he sat down on the floor next to her. "Look, when I say 'every second counts', that doesn't mean you should try to stay one step ahead of time. Time passes whether you like it or not, Anna. That's what makes life worth living. The tick-tock of time reminds you to enjoy the moment you're in.

Never wish a moment away, because you'll never get that moment again."

"That's what you think," Anna sighed. Then her dad gave her a hug and Anna felt better than she had in ages. "Thanks, Dad," she said softly. "See you again soon."

"Again? You mean after school?" asked Anna's dad.

08:02:56.

"Not exactly," replied Anna, looking at her watch. "You're going to tell me to make sure I catch that bus in three ... two ... one ..."

08:03:00.

"Make sure you catch that bus," said her dad. "Remember, every second counts ..."

Sure enough, Anna was standing in front of the door. Her hand was reaching for the door handle yet again. Anna looked down and spotted her watch – the one with the red strap – on her wrist. She took it off and threw it over her shoulder.

Not this time, she thought. Anna had had enough of time altogether. Or, at least, she'd had enough of watching time ... checking time ... being ruled by time.

Tick-tock, tick-tock ...

Maybe her brother had been right all along – maybe she had got stuck counting every second even before she was trapped in this same maddening minute.

Maybe it was time not to care so much about time.

In that moment, Anna vowed that if she ever got out of this minute, this same sixty seconds, she would try to bother less about being on time, every time.

But first she needed to escape. One last attempt to catch the bus.

One last minute ...

Chapter 10
One Last Minute

"I'm free!"

08:02:03.

Anna Gain knew this next minute inside and out. Every second, every moment. Anna suddenly felt rather calm.

First things first, she thought. She dug her brother's shoe out from under the stairs and handed it to him.

"How did you know where it was?" asked Anna's brother.

"Tell you later – I hope," Anna said. Then she grabbed an umbrella from the shoe cupboard and headed for the front door. She waited a moment before she turned the handle. With a deep breath, Anna pulled open the door.

08:02:06.

"Morning, Pandora," Anna said to Mrs Crimp's cat as it lay in the sun. She walked down the path and picked Pandora up. "Let's make sure no one treads on you for the next fifty seconds, shall we?" Anna added. "Let's take you home."

Anna tucked the cat under her left arm, took three steps down the path and swung open the front gate. Old Mr Upshot gave her a wave from the other side of the road as he walked his dopey Doberman.

"It's a—" Mr Upshot began to say.

"—Morning for yawning!" Anna shouted.

"I was about to say the very same thing ..."
the old man muttered. A moment later, his
dog, who had not spotted that Mrs Crimp's cat
was there in the crook of Anna's elbow, barked
instead at the pigeon, which flew from the tree.

08:02:12.

"Right on time," Anna said as the pigeon
flew over her head. She opened the umbrella
as Late Kate rode towards her on her bicycle.

"Kate, you're going to need this!" Anna
shouted, and handed the umbrella to Late Kate
as she sped past. A confused Late Kate held the
umbrella above her head. Little did she know it
was about to protect her from a nasty case of
pigeon-poo-on-the-head.

With Late Kate safely on her way, Anna
ducked the butterfly as it fluttered around her
face. The Number 13 bus rumbled past her. All
she had to do was take the twelve steps to the
bus stop.

08:02:26.

"I can make it ..." Anna said. Her brother ran past her as the bus pulled up. Its doors hadn't even opened. "I can actually make it this time!"

Anna began to run. Every other time, something else had gone wrong. But this time, Anna was almost close enough to the bus to touch it. This time, Anna *had* time. This time, she'd thought of everything.

Then she heard Mrs Crimp's voice echo up the road:

"Pandora! Brekkies, Pandora!"

08:02:35.

Anna looked down at her arms.

She was still carrying the cat.

"Oh no," she muttered. "Pandora! No, no, no!"

08:02:40.

Even as Anna raced *past* the bus and down the road to Number 44, she couldn't believe she'd been so stupid. She skidded to a halt and pushed Pandora into Mrs Crimp's arms just as the bus's doors opened with a *SHUFF*. Anna looked back to see her brother step onto the bus.

Anna *ran*.

She raced up the pavement as fast as her legs could carry her, holding her breath as her school bag rapped against her back.

08:02:47.

"Hold the bus!" Anna panted as she ran. The look on her brother's face as he climbed onto the bus said it all – she wasn't going to make it. She was too late. Anna closed her eyes as she heard the doors close with a SHH— And held out her arms.

08:02:56.

"Whuh ...?"

Anna opened her eyes and there was her brother staring back at her from inside the bus. Anna was holding the bus doors open with outstretched arms.

"I said ... hold the bus," Anna puffed.

"Just in time," said the bus driver.

"Am I ...?" Anna said. She went to check her watch but then remembered she'd taken it off. "Did I make it? What time is it?"

The bus driver checked his watch.

"It's three minutes past eight," he replied, looking over at Anna's brother. "And the longer we talk, the later it is."

"*Three* minutes?" Anna repeated. "Three minutes past eight and how many seconds? How many?"

The bus driver raised his eyebrow and checked his watch again.

"Five ... six ... *some*," he replied.

"Some ... seconds!" Anna gasped. "Are you sure? Are you really, really sure?"

"I'm sure of two things," the bus driver replied. "Tomorrow, I will be driving this bus again and trying to forget my dream of being the world's greatest trapeze artist. And two, as sure as sugar lumps, it is currently three minutes past eight in the morning."

"I didn't go back ..." Anna muttered softly. She let go of the doors and looked down at her hands. "I'm *free*!"

"And I'm very happy for you – whatever you're on about," replied the bus driver. "So what are you waiting for? Time's ticking on. Are you getting on this bus or not?"

Anna waited as she remembered the vow she had made at the last minute. She took a deep long breath of morning air and smiled at her brother.

"Thanks," Anna said. "But maybe next time."

Chapter 11
Watching the World Go By

"Every second counts."

Anna watched the bus pull away and vanish down the road. Her brother looked out of the bus's back window and waved. He looked very puzzled. Anna smiled and waved back. She wasn't sure if she was going to explain everything to him – or even if he'd believe her if she did – but she was sure he'd be happy that she was less bothered about being on time.

Anna took a few moments to watch a blue butterfly flutter through the air.

"Every second counts," she said. At last she understood what her dad meant. Time wasn't something Anna had to stay ahead of … time was a gift. Every moment was precious because – *hopefully* – it would never come again.

So Anna waited. She waited and watched the world go by until the next bus came along.

As it turned out, Anna Gain still made it to school in time. In fact, she got to her classroom a minute before the morning bell rang. Then she began to think: what if she'd waited for the bus after that? Would she still have made it to school before the bell? Could she beat the clock?

There was only one way to find out …

Our books are tested
for children and young people by
children and young people.

Thanks to everyone who consulted on
a manuscript for their time and effort in
helping us to make our books better
for our readers.